Ellie's Room

by

Kathryn Lynn Seifert

illustrated by Ann Murray

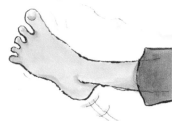

For anyone who ever felt a bit disorganized. K.S.
For R.M., the most organized person I know. A.M.

Children's books by Kathryn Lynn Seifert and illustrated by Ann Murray:

<u>Penelope: The Adventures of a Penny</u>
<u>Hank the Hanger</u>

Word skills game:

<u>Word Dissection</u>

The illustrations in this book were created using Dr. Ph. Martin's watercolor dyes, Blick's Master synthetic bristle brushes, pen and ink, and cotton rag paper. Recycled materials were used for the initial sketches for this book and for the cover art.

This is a work of fiction. Names, characters, places and incidents are either products of the author's and illustrator's imaginations, or if real, are used fictitiously.

With bulging eyes, we gasped at the sight before us! There were clothes draped over bedposts, lamps, and doorknobs. Wrappers littered the base of the already overflowing garbage canister. Then... could it be? Yes... a sock lying all by itself!

1

I nudged my twin sister Sandy. She shrieked! Sandy then tugged on me and whispered, "There's another one all by itself... look over there by the closet, Sam."

Sandy and I will never forget that day... the day we met Ellie *and* her room. Ellie's mom dangled us in the air while calling for Ellie. "Ellie, I thought these would be perfect for you to wear for Crazy Sock Day next Friday."

3

Ellie flipped her book shut and jumped off her bed. Reaching out to grab us, she cried, "Mom, they're great!"

4

Snatching a pair of scissors from her drawer, she snipped us apart. Sandy dropped to the ground. I was pulled onto Ellie's foot. Then it was Sandy's turn. Ohhh... were we stretched!

5

Ellie looked down at us with a huge smile on her face. I think she liked us! "Ellie, why don't you save them to wear for Crazy Sock Day?" Ellie *really* wanted to wear them, but knew her mom was right.

I was peeled
off Ellie's foot first
and tossed onto a pile
of her doll clothes. Then
it was Sandy's turn. She flew
through the air, hit the wall,
and slid behind Ellie's
bed.

7

A few days passed. Every time
Ellie came into her room, I would
watch anxiously. I hoped Ellie would
notice me and then try to find Sandy.

However, each day Ellie's room became more cluttered. Books were piling up on the side of her bed. Colorful beads of different shapes and sizes were strewn about. Dirty clothes were scattered everywhere. Wrappers of all sorts were piled here and there. What if... what if Ellie's room became covered under all her stuff???

9

Friday morning soon arrived. When Ellie woke up, she ran downstairs yelling, "Mom, today is Crazy Sock Day!" "Yes, it is!" smiled her mom. Spinning around, Ellie bolted up the stairs two at a time.

She sprang into her room and
began tossing clothes, toys, and
books this way and that. She spotted
me and leaped over to grab
me. I knew she was happy
to find me... her grasp
was quite tight!

11

"Come on down for breakfast, Ellie," Mom shouted from the bottom of the stairs. "I'll be down soon, Mom," she breathlessly answered. Ellie continued whipping things this way and that. Where could her other crazy sock be?

12

"The bus will be here in 15 minutes," reminded her dad from the upstairs bathroom. Ellie was getting more frantic by the second. She had been anticipating this day since her school principal announced it. Where was her other sock?

13

Now... "It's time to come down now," Mom stated firmly. Ellie knew she had no time left to look. She tossed me on her dresser and grabbed a pair of white socks from her drawer. After slipping them on, Ellie slumped downstairs.

14

She slurped down her cereal, slid her toothbrush over her teeth, ran her fingers through her hair, grabbed her backpack and yelled, "Love you," to her dad and mom. Sprinting to the bus, Ellie made it just in time.

On the bus ride, she found the first open seat and plopped down with her head hung low. She tried to look only out the window, but couldn't help take a quick look at the other kids' socks. They were all colors and designs, but Ellie thought hers would have been the best.

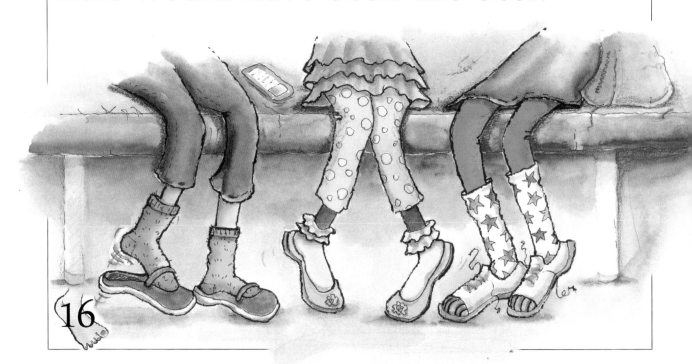

Ellie didn't have them on, though, so no one would ever know. She stared out the window all the way to school.

17

When the bus pulled into the bus ramp and all the children climbed off, Ellie's friends asked where her crazy socks were. Ellie looked down and muttered, "I couldn't find them." Although Ellie felt sad, she complimented all the children's crazy socks that day because she knew that was the right thing to do.

On the bus ride home, Ellie thought about her messy room. If she were more organized, she knew she would have had her socks together and ready to wear to school that day.

19

When Ellie arrived at home, her mom greeted her at the door. Ellie looked up at her mom and asked if she would help her organize her room. She tearfully whimpered how she wished she could've found her other crazy sock. She told her mom how they were definitely the craziest of all she had seen that day.

20

Ellie's mom said, "Yes, let's start right now by making a chart. Every night before you get ready for bed, it's important that you do everything on the chart." Her mom took paper out of the drawer and asked Ellie what she thought should be on the chart.

Ellie's Checklist

— Every toy and book placed back in its spot

— All garbage in garbage canister (and emptied when full)

— Dirty clothes in hamper

— Outfit (socks, too!) laid out for next day

22

When the chart was finished, they both went upstairs and did exactly what the chart stated. As Ellie was looking under her bed, she found Sandy. "Mom, here's my other sock!" She immediately picked me up off her dresser and put me in her drawer along with Sandy. We were together once again.

23

Sandy and I had a feeling that Ellie would take much better care of us now that she had a plan in place. And, even when we are being worn by Ellie, we know each other is just a step away!

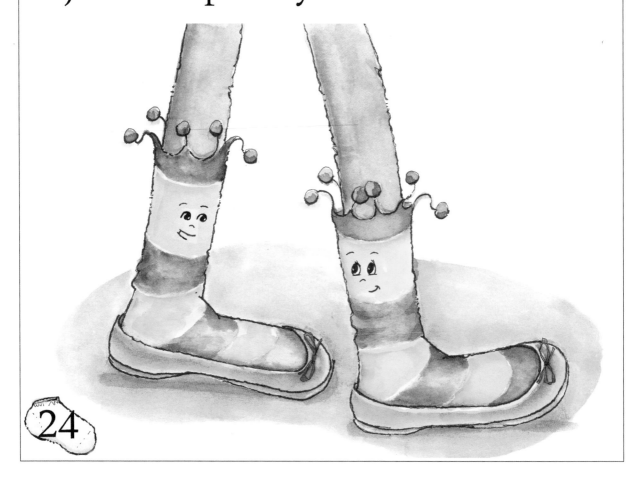